Pocket's Christmas Wish

For Sam and his MoMo,
with love, joy, memory, promise, and comfort. – A.B.

Merry Christmas Francesca and Isabel, love from Daddy xx – R.J.

English language edition for the United States and Canada
published in 2010 by Barron's Educational Series, Inc.

The Americanization of *Pocket's Christmas Wish*, originally published in the UK in 2009,
is published by agreement with Oxford University Press.

All inquiries should be addressed to:
Barron's Educational Series, Inc.
250 Wireless Boulevard
Hauppauge, New York 11788
www.barronseduc.com

ISBN-13: 978-0-7641-6352-4
ISBN-10: 0-7641-6352-3

Library of Congress Control No.: 2010922862

Date of Manufacture: July 2010
Manufactured by: Printplus Limited, Shenzhen, China

9 8 7 6 5 4 3 2 1

Pocket's Christmas Wish

Ann Bonwill & Russell Julian

BARRON'S

On Christmas morning, just outside their burrow,
five rabbits met a snow angel.

Four rabbits hopped ahead to the skating pond,
but Pocket, the littlest rabbit, stayed behind.
He had a question to ask.

"Excuse me," said Pocket. "Can you tell me the meaning of Christmas?" But the snow angel didn't answer.

Pocket wrinkled his bunny nose. He twitched his bunny ears.
He wiggled his bunny whiskers. The snow angel sparkled in
the lemon light, but still she didn't answer.

A trail of footprints led away from the snow angel's skirt. It stretched as far as Pocket could see. "I wish I knew the meaning of Christmas," thought Pocket. "Maybe if I follow the footprints, I'll find it at the end."

And off he hopped.

The footprints wound around the edge of the skating pond.
Pocket paused to watch his brothers and sisters
swooshing and spinning together on the ice.

In their bunny smiles Pocket could see the love of family.
But the footprints didn't stop at the pond, so Pocket hopped on.

Pocket followed the footprints to a holly bush where a little bird was trilling and chirping among the berries. As he listened to the merry music, Pocket could hear the joy of song.

But the footprints zig-zagged away from the bush,
so Pocket hopped on.

The footprints led Pocket to a clearing in the forest where the air was thick with the scent of coming snow. As he sniffed the air, Pocket could smell the memory of winters past. But the footprints made a loop around the clearing and tiptoed out the other side.

Pocket still wished he could find the
meaning of Christmas, so he hopped on.

Pocket followed the footprints to a fallen log.
It was starting to snow. He caught the dancing flakes
on his pink bunny tongue. They tasted fresh,
like the promise of something new.

But the footprints didn't stop at the log,
so Pocket hopped on.

Up ahead, a pine tree grew tall and strong. Pocket sat under its branches to rest his tired bunny feet. The carpet of pine needles felt soft, like the comfort of home. He wished he could stay and rest awhile, but the footprints weren't resting, so Pocket hopped on.

Pocket was cold. The wet snow coated his bunny nose
and ears and clung to his bunny whiskers. Pocket
was hungry. But he couldn't eat the grass that was tucked
beneath the snow for the winter. Pocket wondered
how he was supposed to find the meaning of Christmas
with a rumbling tummy and icy whiskers.

He plodded on, down a hill and across a stream, until he came to a small cottage with a dark red door. The footprints ended.

Pocket peered through the cottage window. He saw three children gathered around a tree with twinkling lights.

He heard their happy laughter and smelled the woodsy
smoke of their log fire. He even tasted the faint flavor
of cinnamon wafting out of the cracks around the
window frame. The snow under Pocket's feet
didn't feel so cold any more.

Then the dark red door opened, just a sliver, and a fat,
orange carrot appeared. Pocket hopped over to the carrot
with his mouth watering, but as he started to nibble,
a baby wood mouse scurried out from under the sled.

The mouse looked cold.
The mouse looked hungry.
The mouse looked up at Pocket
with round mouse eyes.

As he shared the carrot with the mouse, Pocket knew
the gift of giving. At last his wish had come true.
He had found the meaning of Christmas.

Pocket hopped home,

his heart full

of love,

joy,

memory,

promise,

and comfort.

The gifts of the Christmas season.

When Pocket reached the skating pond, his brothers
and sisters were just coming off the ice. As soon as
they saw him, they shook their bunny tails and
thumped their bunny feet.

"Merry Christmas!" said Pocket,
as he chased them back to the burrow.

And it was.